Star of the SHOW

J.M. Klein

An imprint of Enslow Publishing

WEST **44** BOOKS™

The **TOTALLY** SECRET DIARY of DANI D.

New School, New Me!

My Home Is a Battlefield

Star of the Show

Best Friends For-Never

Please visit our website, www.west44books.com.
For a free color catalog of all our high-quality books,
call toll free 1-800-542-2595 or fax 1-877-542-2596.

Cataloging-in-Publication Data

Names: Klein, J.M.
Title: Star of the show / J.M. Klein.
Description: New York : West 44, 2020. | Series: The totally secret diary of Dani D.
Identifiers: ISBN 9781538381991 (pbk.) | ISBN 9781538382004 (library bound) |
  ISBN 9781538383001(ebook)
Subjects: LCSH: Children's plays--Juvenile fiction. | Schools--Juvenile fiction. |
  Diaries--Juvenile fiction. Classification: LCC PZ7.K545 St 2020 | DDC [F]--dc23

First Edition

Published in 2020 by
Enslow Publishing LLC
101 West 23rd Street, Suite #240
New York, NY 10011

Editor: Theresa Emminizer
Designer: Seth Hughes

Photo credits: cover (faces) Arkadivna/iStock/Thinkstock.

Printed in the United States of America

CPSIA compliance information: Batch #CS18W44: For further information contact
Enslow Publishing LLC, New York, New York at 1-800-542-2595.

The TOTALLY SECRET DIARY of

DANI D.

This diary belongs to...

Dani Donaldson
(Don't call me Danielle!)

Age 11

Favorite Foods
Extra chocolaty brownies and PIZZA!

Favorite Color
Purple

Favorite Animal
Horses

Likes
Making extra chocolaty brownies with Dad. Writing in my diary. Movie nights. Making crafts. Watching *Dance For It!* on TV. DANCING!!!

Tuesday, February 5

The Pirate Queen.

That's the name of the new school play. *The. Pirate. Queen.*

Titles are important. They tell you if something is going to be stupid. Or if it's going to be cool. And *The Pirate Queen* tells you SO much. It tells you the play is going to be about an awesome girl. Who is a pirate AND a queen.

A pirate and a queen! A girl who is the boss! I can't imagine anything better than that. And neither can any other girl in my middle school.

At school today, that was all anyone could talk about. We got in trouble in science because we weren't paying attention.

"This might be on the test," Mr. Gisi said. I can't remember what he was talking about. "This is very important."

Ha! Like it's more important than *The Pirate Queen*!

Mr. Gisi made us all take notes. He wanted us to "focus." But making us take notes didn't do anything. We still all talked about *The Pirate Queen* at lunch. And in the hallways. And then during math.

"This is going to be so *amazing*," I heard Hailey say. Hailey is usually the star of the school plays. "Mrs. Leonard says we are going to learn how to sword fight!"

Even the boys talked about it. I caught Danny M. talking to Leo and Jayden before English. But they weren't talking about the *interesting* stuff. They didn't talk about the adventures the Pirate Queen leads. Or the sword fights she wins. Or the journey she goes on to save the kingdom. They kept saying "*arrrr*" and "ahoy, matey!" over and over again. It was ANNOYING.

I rolled my eyes at Danny M. "You guys are *so* immature," I told him.

He made a face at me. "I bet *you* want to be the Pirate Queen, Dani D.," he said. "Just like all the other girls. Admit it."

I was NOT going to admit it. Not to Danny M., that's for sure. Danny M. is the most annoying boy EVER. Every day he does something to bug me—all because he has to share a first name with me.

But he was right.

EVERY girl wants to be the Pirate Queen.

Including me.

Wednesday, February 6

Lunchtime at school stinks.

Not because of the eating part. I like the eating part. But because I have to decide where to sit.

I could sit with Rachel. Rachel is nice. But she always makes fun of my favorite TV dance show, *Dance For It!* I could sit with Natalie. Natalie is fun. But she has a crush on Leo. Leo always sits with Danny M. And I am NOT eating at the same table as Danny M!

At my old school, this was no problem. I ALWAYS sat with Emily Grace. Emily Grace is my best friend. We've been best friends since second grade. And my old friends Kayla and Jasmine sat with us, too.

But I haven't seen Emily Grace in almost three months. Not since Mom and I moved. And I don't have a best friend here.

I have *friends*. I have girls I sit next to in

class. I have girls I text with. Or girls I work on school stuff with.

But they aren't *best* friends.

Best friends are different. Best friends are special.

Today at lunch, I sat with Hailey and her friends Tasha and Priya. Hailey said hi when she saw me. Tasha smiled. But then they went right back to talking to each other.

It was like I wasn't even there.

This is how it usually is. I tried being friends with Hailey and Tasha and Priya when I first moved here. Everyone likes Hailey and Tasha and Priya. I thought if I was friends with them everyone would like me. But I lied. I told them I used to be a drama club star at my old school. That's not true. They were hurt when they found out I lied to them. I told them I was sorry. And they said they forgave me. But it's not the same.

Not really.

They are nice. They are friendly. But they don't text me after school. They don't ask me to hang out on the weekends.

Normally, I don't know what to talk to them about. But today, they were still talking about *The Pirate Queen*.

"The costumes are going to be *amazing*," Tasha said. "My mom already said she's going to help."

"I'm so excited," Priya said. "I can't wait to find out who gets to be the Pirate Queen!"

And that's when I said, "I can't wait, too. I *love* the Pirate Queen. She sounds so cool. The show sounds totally amazing."

They all stopped talking. They all looked at me.

Hailey smiled. "Yes, totally amazing. You *have* to come see it, Dani D."

Tasha smiled too. "Yes, you've *got* to, Dani D. It's going to be the best play ever."

I wasn't smiling. Come *see* the play? "Why can't I be in the play?" I asked. "Why can't I be the Pirate Queen?"

Hailey blinked at me for a few seconds. Like she was waiting for me to say I was joking or something.

"You want to be the Pirate Queen?" she asked. "*Really?*"

And then she and Tasha gave each other a *look.* Tasha even raised her eyebrows. They didn't think I could be in the play!

At all!

"I thought you didn't like drama club," Priya said. "You know. Because of What Happened Before."

I started to feel all hot behind my ears. What Happened Before was I tried to play their drama club games at a sleepover. I had no idea how to play them. I wasn't very good at them. That's when they all found out I had lied about being a drama club star.

"I like drama club," I said. "Really."

They didn't look like they believed me.

At all.

"It's okay, Dani D.," Tasha said. "Acting isn't for everyone. You had a hard time with the drama club games we played at the sleepover. Plays are worse. If you have stage fright, it wouldn't be fun for you."

She said all this like she was trying to do me a favor. Like she was trying to be nice.

She probably was.

That made it even worse. She felt sorry for me. I don't want Tasha to feel sorry for me. I want Hailey and Tasha and Priya to think I *do* have talent.

I want them to think I'm someone they can still be friends with.

I started to feel like I was going to cry. I did NOT want to cry in front of Hailey or Tasha or Priya. Not again. I did that at the sleepover too.

So I told everyone drama club games were NOT the same as being in a play. I said it was totally different.

That better be true.

Because that's when I did it.

I told them I was going to try out for *The Pirate Queen*.

Thursday, February 7

I think I'm going to be sick.

I'm right by the school theater. At the tryout sign-up sheet. Only instead of signing up, I am sitting on the floor writing in my diary.

Because I think I'm going to be sick.

Really.

Sometimes Mom says I just need to calm down. She says, "You are going to be fine, Dani. You are not really going to be sick. You just need to take a deep breath."

I'm taking deep breaths. Lots and lots of them. And I *still* feel sick.

I did not think I would be this nervous. All I have to do is write down my name! I didn't think I would be nervous *at all*.

All day long, I daydreamed about being the Pirate Queen. My daydream made school so much better. I HATE sitting still in class. It makes me feel all itchy and trapped. It's the WORST part about school. Well, that and Danny M.

But in my daydream, I got to MOVE. I got to be on stage instead of sitting still. It was like being in my favorite dance show. People clapped and cheered for me. Everyone thought I was special. Everyone thought I was important. And everyone wanted to be my friend.

The Pirate Queen doesn't worry about best

friends. Everyone wants to be HER friend. I bet if I were the Pirate Queen I wouldn't NEED a best friend.

I would be too busy being the star of the show.

But then I got to the sign-up sheet. And now everything does not feel great.

Everything feels new. And scary. Tasha is right. I've never done drama club before. I couldn't even play drama club games!

And the sign-up list is SO LONG. Every girl must have already signed up. Any of them could end up playing the Pirate Queen. Not me. I could get stuck playing something stupid. Like a sea turtle. And Hailey and Tasha would look at me again like they are sorry for me.

Oh! There's another girl here. I think she wants to sign up too. I'm in her way. I'd better move.

Still Thursday

The girl's name is Paige.

I don't have any classes with her. But I've seen her around school. She is always smiling and laughing. She's tiny and has short dark hair. She looks like a fairy princess. I told her that. And she loved it!

"Thank you," she said. "That's who I want to be in the play! The fairies who help the Pirate Queen are really cool."

This was GREAT news. Paige didn't want to be the Pirate Queen! At least there's one girl I don't have to worry about.

Paige sat next to me on the floor. She didn't think it was weird I was sitting there. Or at least, she didn't ask me why.

"Is that your diary?" she asked. "The cover is so pretty."

I told her all about how my dad gave me the

diary when Mom and I moved here. She got so excited. She bounced up and down. Just like I do! Paige has a sketchbook her dad gave her. She draws instead of writing. Her parents are already divorced. They split up two years ago.

"My parents are getting divorced *right now*," I told her.

"Ugh, parents are the *worst*," Paige said. "Did yours fight all the time? About stupid stuff?"

"Yes!" I said. It was like she totally knows my parents. "All the time. About the weirdest stuff."

"*So* weird," Paige says. "My parents got into a fight about buying toilet paper."

She rolled her eyes and laughed. It was pretty funny.

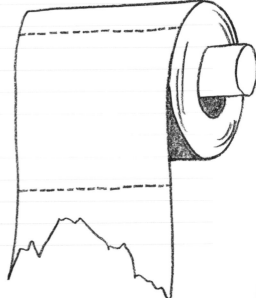

"My parents got into a fight last month at the zoo about water bottles," I said.

She snorted. "It gets easier though. My parents fight less now that they're divorced."

That's what I hoped would happen. My parents do seem like they are fighting less now. But it was really nice to hear it could stay that way. It was really nice to talk to someone else who has gone through the same thing.

This was the first time that's happened to me.

"Are you going to audition for the play?" Paige asked. She said *audition.* Not *try out.* I was even using the wrong words!

"I want to," I said. "I'm really nervous. I've never done anything like this before."

And then I did something surprising—I told Paige all about Hailey and Tasha and Priya.

I told her how they don't think I can be in the play. I told her how I lied about being a drama club star. I told her I have never done theater before. And I told her I have no idea how to be an actress.

And then something even more surprising happened.

Paige wants to help me!

"You should join drama club," she said.

I made a face. She laughed. "No, really. It won't be like the sleepover. I really like drama club. The drama club teacher, Mrs. Leonard, is really nice. We have lots of fun. Next week, we are meeting every day after school. We are going to practice our auditions. If you join drama club, we can get ready for the audition together."

This sounded like a good idea. I could practice first. I could learn how to act. So that way it *won't* be like last time at all.

Besides, being in a play can't be the same as playing those games. Those games were hard. I had to make stuff up. I won't have to make up stuff once I'm in the play. All I have to do is remember lines. That doesn't sound hard at all.

Being the star of the show is going to be SO much easier than drama club games.

"You won't even have to worry about Hailey and Tasha and Priya this week," Paige said. "They don't need to practice. They audition all the time. So they won't be at drama club this week."

That sounded even better! So I did it! I signed up to audition, AND I joined drama club!

This is totally going to work! I will be the Pirate Queen. And once I am the star of the show, I will have lots of friends. Even Hailey and Tasha and Priya will want to be my friends again!

Monday, February 11

DANNY M. IS HERE AT DRAMA CLUB.

I can't BELIEVE this. He's totally here. It's like he's TRYING to ruin all of school for me—even the after-school part!

I'm trying to ignore him. It doesn't matter if he's here. I can ignore him in class. So I can ignore him in drama club.

I CAN. That's why I am writing in my diary now. So it is completely obvious—I AM IGNORING DANNY M.

He keeps glancing my way. Like he thinks I'm going to look at him or something. But I am not going to look at him. I am going to keep writing.

Only it was so much fun before he got here. Paige jumped up and down when she saw me. The way she jumped reminded me of a dance move from last year on *Dance For It!* So I showed the move to Paige. She knew a different dance move. She showed that to me. And then we put them together. We made up a whole new dance!

Everyone else in the room watched and clapped. A couple of girls I didn't know before—Maya and Chloe—even started dancing with us.

It was the most fun ever. It made me feel happy and free. Like I was doing exactly what I was supposed to be doing.

And that's when Danny M. walked into the room.

He came in with the drama teacher, Mrs. Leonard. And that's because he is Mrs. Leonard's assistant. He's the student director. That's why he was talking about the play before.

This totally stinks! If I want to be the Pirate

Queen, I have to work with Danny M.

But I'm not going to let it stop me. I'm not. We're going to read the play out loud next. I already peeked at the script. I LOVE the Pirate Queen. Her lines are even cooler than I thought they would be. She's going to be so much fun to play. Hailey and Tasha and Priya will DEFINITELY be my friends then!

We have to learn a speech tonight. And then tomorrow, we will say the speech in front of everyone else.

"It's a lot of words to learn in one night," Mrs. Leonard told us. "But the girl who plays the Pirate Queen will have to remember *many* lines. So this is a good way to see if you can handle the part."

I'm not worried at all. This is the easy part. I don't have to make anything up. I KNOW I can do this. I'll just keep ignoring Danny M. and learn this speech. And everything will be perfect.

Tuesday, February 12

Learning lines is hard! Much harder than I thought!

I'm in drama club again. We are taking turns saying the Pirate Queen's speech. It's my turn to go next. That means I have to sit still and wait. I hate waiting. I hate sitting still. I just want to dance with Paige. We were dancing at the beginning of class. But we had to stop when Mrs. Leonard came in with Danny M.

"All right, everyone," she said. Danny M. stood right next to her in the front of the classroom. Like he was all important. "I'm really excited to hear all your speeches."

I'm not really excited to say the speech. I stayed up late last night trying to learn it. Mom would probably be mad if she knew how late. I didn't even have time to write in my diary! It was much harder than I thought. But I think it's mostly okay. There are a few sentences I can't say right. And I usually mix up some words. But I'm sure none of that really matters.

Wednesday, February 13

It turns out you can't just sort of learn lines. You have to get EVERY SINGLE WORD right.

Mrs. Leonard is TOUGH. She kept making me say my speech over and over again. "Try again, Dani D.," she said. "Now, try it a little louder. The people in the back of the room have to be able to hear you!"

I tried talking louder. But then Mrs. Leonard said I was talking TOO loud.

"Don't *scream*," she said. "And breathe. You need to remember to *breathe*."

This only made my tongue get all twisted up.

"Now let's try showing a little more emotion," Mrs. Leonard said

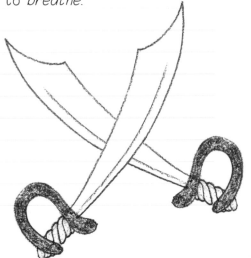

next. "The Pirate Queen is about to go on an important journey. Show how she would *feel*."

I smiled as I said my lines. I tried to show that the Pirate Queen was happy to go on a trip. But Mrs. Leonard didn't look very impressed.

"Acting is more than smiling, Dani D.," she said. "You have to *be* the character. You have to *feel* what she is feeling."

All I felt was really silly.

It was a good thing Paige was there. She made funny faces whenever Mrs. Leonard was talking. That helped. It made me laugh. And that kept me from getting upset in front of Danny M.

Next, we had to pretend to walk like the Pirate Queen would walk. This was easier. I decided the Pirate Queen would walk across the room like she was dancing. I shuffled back and forth. Just like another dance I saw on my show.

Mrs. Leonard got a funny look on her face as she watched me. But Paige and Maya both liked it. They both told me after.

"That was the funniest walk," Maya said. "Will you show me how to do it?"

I showed it to her. Then all three of us danced and danced until our parents picked us up.

"You looked like you were having fun," Mom said on the way home. "It looks like drama club is helping you make friends."

Mom was totally right. My plan is working. I will have lots and lots of friends when I am the Pirate Queen.

Thursday, February 14

I'm sitting at lunch with Paige and Maya!!!

Paige saw me when I walked into the cafeteria. She HOPPED out of her chair.

"Dani!" she called. She jumped up and down. She waved at me. "Over here!"

She didn't even call me Dani D. It was like to her, I was the only Dani here.

So now I'm sitting at their lunch table. And I'm even writing in my diary! Paige and Maya don't mind at all if I write.

"Your diary is cool!" Paige is saying. "You should write. That's important."

Paige is even sketching me while I'm writing. While I'm writing down what she says. Ha! Maya is laughing at us both.

Paige says Danny M. will be in charge of drama club today. *Ewww.* Mrs. Leonard has to do something for the set of the play. We aren't going to listen to Danny M. We are both going to ignore him. We are going to dance instead!

Later Thursday, February 14

Danny M. is kind of ~~cute~~ FUNNY LOOKING when he gets upset. I don't think he likes being ignored. It makes all the freckles on his face stand out. Ha!

Drama club is so much fun when I get to dance with Paige! I think that's the way it should be every day!

Danny M. actually wasn't as bad at being in charge as I thought he would be. I think it's probably because he doesn't have time to be annoying. Everyone is working really hard. This play stuff is a lot of work!

Friday, February 15

Drama club would be SO much harder without Paige and Maya.

Maya is really good at learning lines. She sat with me after school today and helped me. We said my speech over and over again. And that helped a lot.

I almost know the whole speech. That's good. I have to say it at the audition.

Learning lines is just so boring. And hard work. This is not what I thought being the Pirate Queen would be like. At all.

I still like drama club though. It's fun to talk to Maya. It's fun to talk to Paige. It's even fun to ignore Danny M.

Tuesday, February 19

Today is audition day.

I've been having so much fun with Paige and Maya, I sort of forgot about it. But it's already here! It's lunchtime. The audition is after school. That's only a few hours away!

I'm a little nervous. That's what I've been telling Paige and Maya now. But Paige says not to think about it.

"You're totally ready, Dani," Paige is saying.

"You're going to be *great*," Maya is saying.

I *do* know the entire speech I'm supposed to say. Every sentence and every word. In order, too. I've even gotten better at showing emotion, like Mrs. Leonard wants. And I'm used to giving my speech in the drama club classroom in front of Mrs. Leonard. I just have to do the same thing this afternoon.

That's what I'm telling Maya and Paige.

Uh-oh.

I have a BIG PROBLEM.

Maya and Paige just told me that's NOT how the auditions will work. Auditions are in the big theater. NOT the classroom. I have to give my speech in front of EVERYONE. In front of all the kids who are also trying out for the play.

So Hailey, Tasha, and Priya will be there in the theater. Watching me.

I HAVE to do a good job today. I HAVE to get this right. If I don't, I'm going to totally embarrass myself in front of Hailey and Tasha and Priya. Then they will REALLY think I'm not talented. And this time, they won't want to be my friends at all!

Still Tuesday

I'm in the hallway.

My audition did not go well.

At all.

All that work, and I could not remember my speech. I got the words all mixed up. And the more I got the words mixed up, the worse it got.

I got all stiff. My voice dropped. You definitely could not hear me in the back of the theater. You could barely hear me at all. And I didn't show the Pirate Queen's emotion. I only showed *my* emotion—totally scared.

Hailey and Tasha and Priya sat in the second row. They stared at me with their eyes wide. They could totally tell I was struggling. They weren't smiling at how good I was. They weren't thinking I was talented.

They just looked sorry for me.

It made it even worse.

So I just stopped talking. Completely. I stood on the stage like I was the biggest idiot ever. It would have been better if I had run out of the room. Then at least I wouldn't have been in front of all those staring eyes.

Tasha was right. I can't do this play. It's not right for me. At all. I'm not talented. I can't be the Pirate Queen.

I thought it was as bad as it could get. But then Danny M. made it worse.

He stood up. And he said, "Thanks for your speech, Dani D. It would help us now if you could show us a dance."

A dance! He asked me to show them a dance! He was totally making fun of me. He watched Paige and me dance all week. He knows I like to dance. He knows I think dancing is fun. And he waited until I was failing my audition—and he

MADE FUN OF ME.

It was the meanest thing he's ever done.

Hailey and Tasha gave each other another big LOOK. The kind that says they think I'm even weirder than they thought I was. It's awful to have people feel sorry for you. It's awful to be made fun of. And it's awful for someone to take something you love—like dancing—and try to turn it into something bad.

So I just said, "You've already seen me dance this week." And then I walked out of the theater as fast as I could.

I have a whole half hour to wait until Mom picks me up. This stinks. I want to be home where no one can see me. I want to crawl under my blanket. And hide.

I never should have tried out for the play in the first place.

-Still Tuesday

Mrs. Leonard just posted the cast list.

I'm still in the hallway waiting for Mom. So I looked right away.

I'm not the Pirate Queen.

I'm not in the show.

At all.

Still Tuesday

Hailey is going to play the Pirate Queen. That's what the cast list said.

Hailey.

Not me.

I'm back in my room now. Mom tried to cheer me up on the way home. She said we could stop for ice cream. But I told her I wanted to come home. I wanted to write in my diary.

Paige found me right when Mom pulled up.

"I've been looking *everywhere* for you," she said. She gave me a hug. "Are you okay? You looked so sad."

I AM sad. But not because I'm not the Pirate Queen. I think I stopped wanting to be the Pirate Queen a long time ago. She has so many lines to remember. Learning lines is hard. Saying the lines WITH EMOTION is even worse!

I'm sad because I'm not in the play at all. And Paige is in the play. She is going to play the fairy queen. And Maya is another pirate. And a bunch of girls from drama club are other parts.

I didn't tell Paige that. I didn't want to make her feel bad. I just gave her a hug. I told her I would see her tomorrow.

But I'm not actually sure I WILL see her tomorrow.

Play rehearsal is every day after school. Sometimes they even practice during lunch. Paige and Maya are going to be too busy to hang out with me.

I'm going to be the odd person out. They will all be hanging out. Without me.

THAT'S what I'm sad about.

I thought I was going to have lot of friends by being the Pirate Queen. But now I just want to hang out with Paige and Maya. And they are going to be too busy to be my friend.

It feels like losing Emily Grace all over again.

Later Tuesday

The WEIRDEST thing just happened.

It's so weird it feels strange to even write about it. It feels like I'm making up a story. But it's not a story. It totally happened.

Danny M. just came to my house.

DANNY M.

He rang my doorbell. He talked to my mom. He sat on my couch.

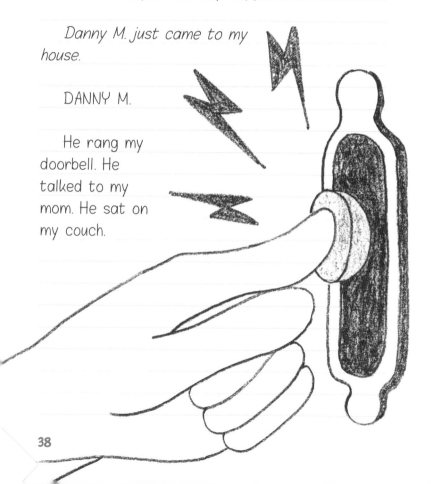

I couldn't believe it. Danny M. Here. IN MY HOUSE.

At first, we both just stared at the carpet. It was strange seeing him outside of school. I didn't know what to say.

Finally he said, "You left the theater without dancing. I wish you would have danced."

This made even less sense than him being here. And then I started to get mad.

"Did you really just come to my house to make fun of my dancing?" I said. "Really? That couldn't just wait until tomorrow?"

His eyes got huge. "What?" he yelped. "No! I'm not here to make fun of you. Really."

I folded my arms and glared at him. It was a pretty good glare, too.

His face turned pink. "I'm not here to make fun of you! I like your dancing. You're really good at dancing."

This was really hard to believe.

"I wanted you to dance because there are dancing parts in the show," Danny M. said. "The queen of the fairies helps the Pirate Queen on her journey. And the fairies are dancers. They don't have any lines. They dance instead of speaking."

It felt like he was telling me I had just won a trip to Disney World. I have *never* been more excited. I wanted to be a fairy dancer more than I have ever wanted ANYTHING. More than I even wanted to be the Pirate Queen.

"Mrs. Leonard has never seen your dancing," Danny M. said. "You've gotten too good at dancing only when the teachers aren't around. So that's why I wanted you to show her."

That's when I realized the problem. "Oh!" I said. "But I didn't dance. So does that mean I can't be a dancer?"

This was like seeing the cast list all over again. Only worse because I had started to hope a little.

"Hold on. Don't get too worked up," Danny M. said. "You always get so worked up."

I frowned. I do NOT get all worked up!

But I didn't have time to argue with him. "Can I still show Mrs. Leonard my dancing? Or is it too late?"

"Mrs. Leonard is deciding on the dancers tomorrow," Danny M. said. "So we need to find a way for her to see your dancing tonight."

This seemed IMPOSSIBLE. But then I remembered Mom had a list of all the teachers' email addresses.

"What if I email Mrs. Leonard a video of me dancing?" I asked. "Do you think that might work?"

He thought it could work! So now Paige is on her way over. She is going to help Danny M. and me make a video. We are going to put all my new dance moves in it. And then we will email it to Mrs. Leonard.

I don't know if it will work or not. But it feels right. Although it's still weird that Danny M. is helping me. I asked him that right now. I said, "Why are you helping me?"

He frowned. "I'm in charge of the show. I want it to be the best it can be. And you are the best dancer at school."

It was the nicest thing anyone has ever said to me. Maybe Danny M. is okay after all. Maybe he's NOT the most annoying boy ever. Maybe he is only annoying SOMETIMES. And maybe he can also be my friend.

MAYBE.

Later later Tuesday

Paige and Danny M. are still at my house!

Mom keeps telling me what time it is. She keeps reminding me about my homework. But I think she doesn't mind too much. She looks happy that I have friends over. She even opened the box of good cookies!

Danny M. ate half the cookies. That WAS annoying. It turns out even when you decide to be friends with people, they can still annoy you. But I guess half a box of good cookies is a small price to pay for all his help.

We are almost finished with the video. Danny M. is finishing it on his phone. He wants it to be a surprise. I'm writing in my diary across from him at the kitchen table to distract myself. Surprises are so hard to wait for!

But making the video was so much fun. Paige and I both danced together. Mom watched. She kept saying, "I didn't know you could dance this way, Dani! You are so good!"

That made me feel really good.

It made me realize I didn't need to be on a big stage like on *Dance For It!* to dance. There doesn't need to be lights. Or a big crowd. That's not what it was about at all.

There just needs to be people who like me, watching me have fun.

Wednesday, February 20

Ugh, I'm SOOO nervous.

We haven't heard from Mrs. Leonard yet. I'm in English class at school. I'm having trouble sitting still. Danny M. keeps poking me with his pencil whenever I move. He says I'm annoying when I can't sit still.

Ha! This whole time I also annoyed Danny M.!

Later Wednesday

The video worked!

I had to wait until after school to find out. That's when Mrs. Leonard posted the list of dancers. And both Paige and I are going to be fairy dancers! Paige gets to dance as queen of the fairies. And I will be the MAIN DANCING FAIRY!! I get to lead the Pirate Queen on her journey! WHILE DANCING!!!!

We both jumped up and down. We squealed and hugged.

"This is the best news ever!" Paige said. "We are going to have so much fun!"

We made so much noise Danny M. came out of the theater. He gave us both a look. "We are trying to have play practice," he said. "You're being really loud."

I frowned at him. He was acting like he did before we were friends.

But then he smiled at me. "Congratulations, Dani D. I think it's really great you get to be a dancer. But you are going to have to work really hard. This part is important. You can't goof around. You have to really practice."

I rolled my eyes at him. Even when he is nice, Danny M. can be ANNOYING. He thinks he is all grown up now. Just because he's in charge. But I still said, "Don't worry. I'm going to work *so hard.*"

And then Paige and I went back to jumping up and down. Then we danced all around again. And when Danny M. told us to be quiet, I said we were practicing for the show. That we had to work. And then he left us alone.

I love my new part!

Even Hailey and Tasha and Priya seemed happy for me. Hailey gave me a hug. "I heard you are a really great dancer, Dani D.," she said. "I'm so excited you are going to be in the play."

That made me feel good. Not as good as celebrating with Paige. But it turns out I didn't really need Hailey and Tasha and Priya to be my best friends. They can still be my friends. But best friends are people who really get you. Best friends are people you *connect* with.

Best friends are people like Paige.

Still Wednesday

I thought I couldn't be any happier than I was at school. But then I got home. Mom said she wanted to talk to me.

At first, I was worried. Mom keeps saying I need to spend more time on my homework. I thought maybe she didn't want me to be a dancer in the play!

"I talked to your dad," she said. I really started to worry then. Mom and Dad don't fight as much as they did before they decided to get a divorce. But they still don't talk much.

"I showed your dad the video of you dancing," Mom said. "We both thought you were great, Dani. But more importantly, we thought you looked really happy. We have a little extra money right now. Would you like to take dance lessons?"

!!!!!!!!!!!

YES!!!! YES I WOULD LIKE TO TAKE DANCE LESSONS!!!

It took me a long time to calm down after that. I leaped and jumped and bounced all around the living room. Mom told me to go write in my diary so that I would sit still.

But she said it with a smile. She laughed. She said, "You know, I think dance is going to be good for something else. You have too much energy to sit still. You need to move around."

That's what I've been saying!!!

The only bad part is, I can't go to drama club anymore. I will be too busy with dance lessons and dance practice for the play. I was a little sad about that. But Maya just texted me. She wants me to go to the movies with her this weekend. And Chloe already asked me to come to her birthday party. So they will still

popcorn

be my friends even if I don't hang out with them every day.

I guess I didn't need to be the Pirate Queen after all to make friends. I didn't need people to think I was special. I didn't need them to think I was important.

I just needed to find my own way. And do my own thing. And make my own friends. And now I do have friends. And I get to dance and move all the time!

And that's SO much better than being the star of the show!

Want to Keep Reading?

Turn the page for a sneak peek
at the next book in the series.

9781538382011

Monday, June 3

I'm so excited. I can't sit still!

I'm in the car with Dad. He's laughing at me. That's because I keep wriggling and squirming— even while writing in my diary.

"I wish I had your energy!" Dad is saying. Then he laughs again when I bounce up and down in my seat.

But I can't help it! In just four hours and thirty-nine minutes, I will be home.

Home!

I will be in my old room. I will be in my old house. And I will see my best friend, Emily Grace. And my old friends Kayla and Jasmine.

How on Earth am I supposed to sit still?!

Mom would find a place where I could get out of the car. She would tell me to dance. That's how I use up energy now. It makes it easier to sit still. But Dad doesn't know that trick. And I am *not* going to tell him.

I want to get home as fast as possible.

Grandma doesn't like it when I call Dad's house "home." She says, "Dani, you live here now. *This* is your home."

That's kind of true. Mom and I have lived in our new town for eight months. We have a new house now. My new room is just the way I like it. I get to take dance lessons. I even have a new best friend, Paige. It does feel like home.

But my old house is still home, too.

That's where my dad lives. Where I learned to ride my bike. Where Emily Grace and I ate a whole tub of ice cream in one night.

And I am going to be there in four hours and thirty-four minutes!

I get to spend the ENTIRE SUMMER at home. I get to see my dad every day. I won't have to video-chat him just to talk to him. I get to hang out with Emily Grace whenever I want. I get to do all sorts of fun things with my old friends.

I can't wait!!!

Dad even has the next week off from work. He's telling me about that now.

"We can do whatever you want," he's saying. "We can go for bike rides. Or make extra-chocolaty brownies. We can watch movies. I'm all yours for the week."

YES! This is so great!

"What would you like to do first?" Dad asks. "There should still be lots of daylight left when we get home."

Oh, wow. There's so much I want to do! It's so hard to decide. Bike rides sound like fun. So does seeing my old room. So does making crafts with Emily Grace. And jumping on the trampoline with Jasmine.

ABOUT THE AUTHOR

J.M. Klein is a former journalist who has lived all around the country and moved half a dozen times. Like Dani, she learned how to make new friends and tried out for the school play. She didn't make that play, but she did develop a lifelong love of theater and now has good friends in many states. She's always written in diaries and journals, the contents of which are still totally secret.

The TOTALLY SECRET DIARY of DANI D.

The TOTALLY SECRET DIARY of DANI D.
New School, New Me!
J.M. Klein

The TOTALLY SECRET DIARY of DANI D.
MY HOME IS A BATTLEFIELD
J.M. Klein

The TOTALLY SECRET DIARY of DANI D.
Star of the SHOW
J.M. Klein

The TOTALLY SECRET DIARY of DANI D.
Best Friends FOR-NEVER
J.M. Klein

Check out more books at:

www.west44books.com